To:

From:

Happy reading!

Chronicles of Coryn:

7 Days of Fun

Coryn Anaya Clarke

ISBN: 9798673116401

Illustrations by Sameer Kassar

To all the children everywhere,

You are beautiful.

You are smart.

You are kind.

You are good.

You are brave.

You are strong.

You are brilliant and one of a kind.

You are important.

For all my friends

Hello, my name is Coryn Anaya Clarke
and I am four years old.

I am from Trinidad and Tobago.

That's a country in the Caribbean.

I love to sing, read and dance,

but do you know what I love most of all?

I love going on adventures and learning new things!

Learning is fun.

Low Crescent Lunge

Lotus

Cobra

4

Today is Sunday.

Do you know what I do on Sundays?

I do yoga!

Yoga is exercise for your body and your mind.

Every week I learn new moves called poses that help me get stronger and more flexible too.

It also helps me relax.

Yoga is a lot of fun.

5

Today is Monday.

On Mondays, I dance.

I'm learning ballet.

Every week, my teacher shows me really cool moves.

I've already learned the plié, relevé, and chassé

but I still need to practice so I can be just as good

as my favourite ballerina.

Her name is Misty.

Did you know that she started dancing

when she was a little girl just like me?

When I grow up I'm going to dance on big stages

just like her.

Today is Tuesday.

On Tuesdays we make music.

I am a singer and musician.

My daddy says I am multitalented.

That means I'm really good at different things.

I'm learning to play three instruments: the piano,

the xylophone, and drums.

The piano is my favourite.

My daddy plays the piano too.

I love when we make music together.

Today is Wednesday.

On Wednesdays, I make yummy treats with my mummy.

Today we're making super moist

red velvet cupcakes with vanilla frosting.

That's my favourite.

My mummy said we can have sweet treats

in mo-de-ra-tion. Moderation!

That means we can have it sometimes but not too much.

11

Today is Thursday.

On Thursdays we swim.

I used to be afraid of the water, but I'm not anymore.

My daddy said learning to swim is especially important

because we live on an island.

Do you know what an island is?

An island is a piece of land surrounded by water.

I live in Trinidad.

Trinidad is an island.

Today is Friday.

On Fridays, I get creative.

Today I am painting a flower garden.

Sunflowers are my favourite.

I love them because they are beautiful,

yellow and bright!

What's your favourite flower?

Today is Saturday.

On Saturdays, I usually go to church and spend time

doing fun things with my family.

Because of the coronavirus, we have to worship at home.

Home church is fun, but I miss the awesome music at real church.

Today we're going to learn about Jonah.

Do you know who he is?

Jonah was swallowed by a whale for disobeying God.

The whale didn't eat him up,

it just swallowed him whole and then spit him out.

Isn't that crazy?

My mummy says that what happened to Jonah teaches us the

importance of being obedient.

And so ends seven days of fabulous fun.

That was amazing wasn't it?

I hope you enjoyed it just as much as I did.

I loved them all.